For Brad, Daisy, and Jonah ... my greatest inspiration.—J.A.K.

For Armen, who helped.—M.S.

Distributed in the United States by NorthSouth Books, Inc., New York 10016.
Library of Congress Cataloging-in-Publication Data is available.
ISBN: 978-0-7358-4218-2
Printed in Latvia by Livonia Print, Riga, October 2016.
1 3 5 7 9 · 10 8 6 4 2
www.northsouth.com

the Green Umbrella

Story by **Jackie Azúa Kramer**

pictures by **Maral Sassouni**

North South

One rainy day an Elephant was taking a walk with his green umbrella.

Along came a Hedgehog.

"Excuse me." said the Hedgehog. "I believe you have my boat."

"Your what?" asked the Elephant.

"I crossed deep oceans on my boat and faced the crash of icy waves. I saw dolphins leap two by two and tasted the salty spray of whales. The stars were my guide and my boat a faithful friend." said the Hedgehog.

"I'm sure you're mistaken," replied the Elephant. "This isn't your boat. It's my umbrella. However, you're welcome to share it and stay dry."

Along came a Cat.

"Excuse me," said the Cat. "I believe you have my tent."

"Your what?" asked the Elephant and the Hedgehog.

"I studied plants and flowers in wooded forests.
In the evenings, among hanging vines and giant leaves,
I'd camp under my trusty tent and enjoy a cup of tea,"
said the Cat.

"I'm sure you're mistaken." replied the Elephant.
"This isn't your tent. It's my umbrella. However. you're
welcome to share it and stay dry."

Along came a Bear.

"Excuse me," said the Bear. "I believe you have my flying machine."

"Your what?" asked the Elephant, the Hedgehog, and the Cat.

"I flew through windy skies in my flying machine. I soared through clouds high up in the air and saw Northern Lights glimmer above rolling hills. I floated on wings free and far from the noise of busy towns below." said the Bear.

"I'm sure you're mistaken." replied
the Elephant. "This isn't your flying
machine or your tent or your boat!
"When I was a child I imagined I was
a pirate and my umbrella was my sword.

"I was a circus acrobat
and my umbrella was
the balancing pole.

"I was a home run hitter and
my umbrella was my bat."

The rain stopped and the sun came out.

"I'll be on my way," said the Elephant closing his umbrella tight. "Good-bye."

"I need my boat!" squealed the Hedgehog.

"I need my tent!" cried the Cat.

"I need my flying machine!" growled the Bear.

Along came an old Rabbit.

"Excuse me," said the old Rabbit. "I believe you have my cane."

"Your what?" asked the Elephant, the Hedgehog, the Cat, and the Bear.

"I climbed hundreds of stairs to the tops of desert pyramids.

"I hiked tall mountains to reach moss covered ruins with the help of my sturdy cane.

"In a maze of dark caves, sure in my steps over stony trails, I discovered ancient treasures," said the old Rabbit.

"I'm sure you're mistaken," sighed the Elephant. "This isn't your cane. It's my umbrella which has sheltered me from the rain and the sun."

The Elephant noticed the old Rabbit wiping his brow from the sun's heat.

"However, you're welcome to share it and stay cool," offered the Elephant opening his umbrella.

"That would be nice," smiled the old Rabbit.

"I can make us all a nice cup of tea!" suggested the Cat.

"Sounds wonderful!" agreed the Hedgehog and the Bear.

So, in the shade of the green umbrella, the Elephant,
the Hedgehog, the Cat, the Bear and the old Rabbit
shared their stories, drank tea, planned adventures,
and became fast friends.

Together they went...
Sailing.
Camping.
Flying.
Hiking.
And when it rained they stayed dry
under the green umbrella.